SASQUATCH'S SEDUCTION

A MF MONSTERLOVER EROTICA

THE CRYPTIDS OF AMERICA
BOOK 1

KATRYNA LALOCK

1

"The best way to get over someone is to get under someone else."

It's what Devan had said to Carmen just two days before, reaching across the table to give her friend's arm a sympathetic squeeze. Devan never liked Elliott; she thought he was pretentious, rude, and – to be honest – not handsome enough for Carmen.

Friends were always that way, weren't they? Assuming you were the sun and the men you associated with were dusty, old moths drawn to something too bright for them to handle. Carmen had tried not to cry at the time; she *hated* crying in public. She held back tears as she nursed her third mimosa during the bottomless brunch. It was an emergency girls' meeting after Elliott cheated on Carmen and blamed it on her.

On the drive home, Carmen had thought over

Devan's words as tears streamed down her face, obscuring her vision. Hastily, she'd wiped them away on her shoulder, both hands tightening on the steering wheel. The brunch had been much needed, but it hadn't filled the giant hole in her heart. After brunch, Devan had caught Carmen's arm before they parted ways.

"Here," she'd said, pressing a piece of paper into Carmen's hand. "This will get you what you need."

Carmen had opened the paper, reading the instructions as if in a daze. "A campsite?" she'd asked, her brow furrowed.

Devan had smiled, her eyes far away as she nodded. "Yes, a campsite. A remote one in Rocky Mountain National Park. It's not *strictly* a campsite." She'd given her friend a conspiratorial wink, her eyes twinkling with mischief.

Carmen nodded mutely and shoved the paper into her pocket.

A few days later, as she emptied her pockets looking for her mail key, she remembered the paper. She flattened the crumpled paper – her fingers tracing the instructions.

She needed to get away; everything in her apartment reminded her of *Elliott*. Netflix's latest binge-worthy dating show only reminded her of nights curled on the couch, gasping at the dysfunctional couples. He'd sounded so reasonable against that backdrop. All that talk he'd spewed: "Man, if they just went to THERAPY! The cornerstone of any relationship is trust. Honestly, it's like no one communicates anymore."

As if he wasn't lying and cheating at the same time.

Even the stupid decorative pillows she placed on her bed reminded her of him! He'd toss them on the floor and shake his head. "Who are you decorating for?" he'd say before nestling under the covers. No matter how many times she told him to keep them off the floor they ended up there, night after night. Tightening her fist over the paper at the memory that surfaced in her mind, she made her choice.

Carmen packed her overnight bag for a camping trip. It wasn't her first; that's how she'd met Devan and the rest of her friends. She hadn't known a soul when she moved to Fort Collins, Colorado. Through hiking, she'd run into a group of like-minded people who loved the outdoors as much as she did. She'd spent the last three summers working on her Chaka tan line and learning the finer points of instant coffee and campsite meals.

It'd been too long since Carmen solo camped. The last few weeks of constant brunches, time with friends, quick hikes, and long phone calls were great to take her mind off Elliott. She needed to really recharge, to be alone with her thoughts instead of burying.

Tears welled in her eyes as she turned into Estes

Park, heading toward Rocky Mountain National Park. She swiped them away, angry at herself for still being upset weeks after the breakup. In a split decision, she pulled into the parking lot to grab a slice of pie from You Need Pie! It was her favorite place to eat after a long day of hiking in the park. This time she used it as fuel before getting started, settling on a ginger mango slice before entering the park at last.

Devan's instructions were detailed and involved a little bit of off-roading. "Don't worry," the paper said. "It's not on a map. Not because it's illegal, but because it's special." They were the strict leave no trace types; there's no way Devan would have her off-roading through a protected area. Carmen nearly missed the turnoff, reveling at the sound of the tires of her Jeep on a dirt road. She continued to bump along the road, stopping here and there to take pictures on her phone of the snow-capped mountains. It always amazed her that the air could be so cold even in the summer, the mountains still covered with snow. She was from northern Mexico, where summer seemed never to end. This... this was a unique and exotic beauty, like none she'd ever seen before.

The dirt road tapered to a stop at a beautiful camp-site. A fire circle sat in the middle of the small clearing, spectacularly shaded by a large tree. A tributary gurgled just a few feet from the clearing. Small bushes edged the clearing, their branches heavy with ripe berries. It was perfect, and for the first time in weeks, Carmen's heart soared. She turned her Jeep around so the trunk opened to the clearing and unloaded her tent and supplies.

Once her Jeep was emptied, Carmen reclined in the folding chair she brought, listening to the music of nature – the bubbling tributary, the sound of birds chirping, the wind delicately stroking the tree overhead. Despite the heavenly silence, Carmen couldn't help but shake the feeling of eyes on her, watching her every movement.

2

The following morning dawned crisp and beautiful. Carmen spent the time tending to her small campsite and making oatmeal. She burrowed in her sleeping bag in the hammock she'd erected between two trees on the edge of the campsite, enjoying a racy romance novel. She had zero signal on her phone, but it didn't matter; her trusty old e-reader kept her well entertained with the books she had downloaded before the trip. She passed her morning like that, relaxing in the hammock and listening to the birds chirp.

By the afternoon, it was downright warm. She shucked off the sleeping bag and eyed up the water. It couldn't have been over ten feet across, and it looked like it had some deeper spots. She considered putting on a bathing suit, but the location was so remote she decided she didn't need it. She peeled off her clothes and tossed them aside, grabbing her camp sandals and slipping them on as she left the campsite shade for the edge of the water.

The water wasn't as cold as she thought it was. It was refreshing compared to the heat of the sun and the warmth of the sleeping bag. She groaned as her tired feet soaked in the water. It took her a while to get accustomed to the coolness. She swam to the center of the tributary, and floated on her back, letting the sun warm her naked body. Carmen cracked an eye open, half expecting to see someone at the water's edge watching her. She laughed at herself, remembering how remote this place was.

With that assurance, she slid her hand down her naked body, stopping at her right breast. She circled her brown nipple with her fingers. Her nipples were already perked from the cold water; it didn't take much to encourage them to stand up even taller. She rested just above her waiting pussy after her left hand made a lazy circle down her stomach.

She paused here, not because she was afraid of being caught, but because her mind was blank. Usually, this is where she thought about Elliott, picturing his hand tracing its way down her body, squeezing and kneading all the while. If she were honest with herself, she would admit that he never satisfied her the way her own hands did, a thought that made her frown and nearly squashed her mood.

Her mind took a sharp detour; instead of Elliott, she imagined what would happen if she were truly caught like this in the river. The only people who'd find her out here would be a fellow hiker or, even better, a park ranger. Her eyes fluttered and closed again as she pictured an old park service truck turning down her path, stopping at the end of the road she took. She imagined the man to be tall, with a thick beard and tanned skin that smelled like body wash and the outdoors, hopping out of his truck and heading toward her Jeep to check on her.

He'd come around the end of her truck and see her floating in the water, one hand tweaking her right nipple, the other rubbing her clit in slow circles. She liked that slow burn, the sensation light enough to tease but not enough to send her toward erotic pleasure and the build-up of how it only heightened her inevitable orgasm.

The park ranger wouldn't interrupt her; he'd watch in fascination as she continued, finally dipping a finger into her pussy, bucking her hips just above the water to afford him a look at her. He'd see her thick thighs from years of hiking and marvel at her dark, brown skin gleaming with a sheen of the river water. He should turn away and stop staring at her, but he wouldn't be able to. He'd feel himself harden in his pants. He'd reach down to adjust his cock in his pants but find even that brief movement was enough to set him off. Reservation aside, he'd unbuckle his belt, unzip his pants, and slide them down just enough to free his cock. He'd bring it to its full length with easy strokes along his shaft, capturing a bit of pre-cum from the tip to moisten it.

Carmen's brow furrowed as she added a finger to her wanting pussy, removing her other hand from her nipples to strum her neglected clit. She was more insistent this time, pressing harder on it, the sensation reverberate up her body in a delicious tingle. This is when she'd open her eyes and meet the hungry gaze of the park ranger standing just a few feet away from her now. He didn't realize it in his horny reverie, but he'd slowly been walking closer and closer to her, his hand moving steadily over his shaft.

He'd freeze as their eyes meet, hand stopping at the base of his cock, squeezing in surprise. His surprise would mount when she didn't stop, her mouth partially open, her tongue darting out to moisten her lips. He'd take one, no, two tentative steps toward her, and still, she wouldn't turn him away, still wouldn't yell at him to leave. Emboldened, he'd cross the distance to the shore and kick off his boots, tearing off his socks and pants shortly afterward. She'd laugh as he fumbles for the buttons on his shirt, trying to get as naked as she was in as little time as possible. Now naked, he'd plunge into the river, shivering from the coldness.

He'd be at her side in a few quick and short strides, the water just above his waist at its deepest point. Carmen, sitting upright then, her eyes would only reach his collarbone because of his height. He'd hungrily grab the back of her head, bringing her mouth to his to devour it, tasting like spearmint gum, fresh and minty in her waiting mouth. His other hand would travel down her back to grope her ass, moaning in her mouth when he got a handful of her flesh, pulling her closer. His erection pressing against her torso would shrink a little in the cold water. The hand on the back of her head would move to join his other, scooping her up to wrap her legs around his waist.

He'd be strong; she would know by how easily he lifted her and carried her to the river's edge. In a few more strides, he's carried her to her Jeep, planting her ass on the hood without ceremony. He'd stop their kisses long enough to take her bottom lip into his mouth and gently drag it as if testing her boundaries. She'd groan into his mouth, causing him to smile.

He wouldn't bother to tease her; just kneel in front of her and throw her legs over his shoulders, diving right into her waiting pussy. His tongue would part her folds, sucking a lip at a time into his mouth, his teeth scraping the sensitive flesh. Once she's parted, he'd practically feast on her. His tongue would circle her clit, sucking it into his mouth. He'd nearly bring her to the edge, but she'd hold back, wanting to feel him inside her when she cums. His tongue, inching lower, would probe her opening, groaning at her taste mixed with the river's fresh water. He'd let out a breathy curse, or was it her that curses? Before sliding back up to her clit, he'd linger there a moment before stopping.

The feeling of his mouth no longer on her leaving her empty, her eyes would pop open, trying to understand why he stopped. He'd grab her waist to slide her off the hood before flipping her over, her breasts flush with the Jeep hood, her legs spread, and her pussy exposed. He'd run the head of his cock along with her opening, wetting it with the juices now flowing down the inside of her leg, a mix of his saliva and her own need. He wouldn't tease long, clear he's nearly at the edge himself.

He'd start slowly, pushing just the head of his cock into her. Pausing there, his forehead lowering against her shoulder, she'd feel his breath as he tried to catch it, trying to stop himself from plowing into her.

"Do it," she would groan into the Jeep's hood. "Fuck me like you mean it."

He would need no further prompting. With a quick thrust of his hips, he'd bury himself deep inside her pussy, his balls tightening against her. He'd stop only for a second before thrusting again; one hand on the Jeep's hood near her head, the other wrapped around her so he could furiously rub her clit. This stranger, this person she'd never seen before, would seem to know exactly what to do. He'd circle and flick her waiting bud just the right way, and she would feel an orgasm not far away.

He'd pick up his pace even more, knowing she was just as close as he was.

She would cum first because this park ranger knew precisely how to satisfy her. He would slow his fingers down just enough to push her through an intense orgasm that made the edges of her vision darken. Just a few short pumps behind, he'd bury his entire length into her as he came.

Carmen jolted back into reality as her orgasm washed over her in the river at the same time as her imaginary park ranger. She cried out because why not? Who was there to hear her? Her orgasm overtook her, three fingers deep in herself, her other hand furiously rubbing her clit. She rode her hand wantonly in a way she'd never dared, even in her own bedroom's solace. Being out here alone was freeing, like she'd finally been allowed to be who she was.

She took a few seconds to come down from the orgasm. The slick noise of her fingers sliding out of her pussy was so scandalous she blushed. She stood upright in the water, stretching her arms overhead. That was when she caught movement in the shadows of the bushes around her campsite – something brown and hairy. Her head jerked toward it, but whatever it was had gone by the time she turned to it.

An animal, she reminded herself, laughing. Probably a bighorn sheep, given that it was brown fur she saw. She brought a hand to her forehead and rubbed, laughing to herself. There was no one out here but her and nature.

Right?

3

———

The afternoon was too perfect not to go for a short hike. Carmen spotted a few trails as she drove up the narrow dirt road to the campsite the day before, hikes that begged to be explored. After drying off from her excursion in the river earlier, she covered herself in sunscreen and environmentally safe bug spray, dressed, and tightened her Chaco's. She secured her small hiking backpack with the 3L bladder and started down the dusty trail. She paused before leaving the campsite, wondering if she'd run into the bighorns she'd glimpsed earlier. She trekked back through the campsite to the other side of the bushes, looking for their little hoof prints.

Instead, there was a large footprint. It appeared human, but it was too big to be possible. She placed both feet next to it, marveling at the difference. She pulled out her phone and took a picture of the print next to hers. Was it just some strange bear print warped from by the sand? Or was it from a previous visitor, someone much taller than her?

She tried not to let it bother her as she set down the dirt road to find a hiking trail.

THE SUN SLIPPED BEHIND the mountains just as Carmen returned to camp. She spent the afternoon climbing up the side of the nearest mountain and was rewarded with a sweeping view of the valley below. The park spread out below her like something out of a dream - sweeping valleys bisected by rivers and streams, elk grazing on tall, swaying grass. She snacked on some dried fruit at the top before heading back down.

By the time she got to camp, she was exhausted and starving. She pulled out some quick cook macaroni and cheese, barely waiting for it to cool before she chowed down, burning her mouth in the process. Carmen curled in her hammock, her eyes heavy with exhaustion. The hike, the pleasant summer breeze, and the gentle sway of her hammock were enough to lull her to sleep.

· · ·

THE SOUND of rustling woke Carmen from her sleep. She blinked awake, her eyes straining against the dark of the night. The sun had long since set, and the full moon cast the campsite in a glow. She stretched and yawned, freezing when she heard the noise again – a rustling at the edge of the camp. Her heart hammered in her chest. What if another hiker stumbled on her spot? She was alone with no cell service; how would she call for help if something happened?

She turned slowly to see something even more terrifying than a random hiker. There, its head buried in her food stash, was a bear. And by the looks of it, the bear wasn't very old.

Shit. It was a rookie mistake to leave your food out in the open. She hadn't meant to; she had a bear box in which she kept all her food. She was usually so good about using it, but she'd fallen asleep before putting her food away. Stupid, stupid, stupid! She took a few deep breaths to calm herself. Worst case scenario, they take all her food, and she would leave the next day to get more supplies. The thought of leaving her campsite filled her with sadness, temporarily replacing her dread.

Temporarily.

Another small bear appeared from around her Jeep, sniffing at the tires. Carmen knew well enough what followed two bear cubs. She swallowed hard, trying to sink deeper into the hammock. Maybe they'd catch her scent and leave? Or perhaps they wouldn't see her, and she could hide in the hammock until they were gone? To her mounting horror, one cub wandered toward her hammock. It stood on its hind legs, the moonlight illuminating its black fur. It sniffed the air, its nose crinkling in her direction. Carmen glanced down to the uncovered, unwashed macaroni and cheese container in her lap.

She might as well have smeared herself with honey.

Carmen scoured her mind for what to do when encountering a black bear. Were they the ones you scared away with loud noise? No, she wouldn't dare, especially without having eyes on the mom. If she hid on the edge of the camp and watched her cubs, she'd come running at the first sign of danger. Carmen's best chance was to hold completely still. She shoved the food container under her, trying to stifle the smell.

The bear cub dropped down onto all fours, meandering around the small campsite. Its sibling still rummaged nose-deep in her supplies, rifling around with little success. Carmen was more a fan of quick cook food and freeze-dried things than raw food items. She was a terrible cook and didn't dare make an actual fire during fire season. Hopefully, this would be her saving grace. They would grow bored when they realized how little food she had and leave.

The cub turned its attention to her once more, its nose crinkling as it smelled the air. It came closer and closer to her until its nose bumped the underside of her hammock. Carmen's preference for tying her hammocks higher up in the tree meant she was momentarily safe. The cub needed to stand on its hind legs to see her. That didn't exactly work in her favor as its nose bumped the container she'd shoved under her, which was now more accessible for the bear to sniff. The hammock lurched as a clawed paw brushed at the underside of it. It grunted in anger, its claws pawing more ardently against the fabric.

An answering grunt made Carmen's blood run cold. It was the grunt of a full-grown bear – momma bear. She turned her head a fraction of an inch to see her come from behind the bushes, heading toward Carmen. She had to be at least 100 pounds and, on all fours, was at eye level with Carmen.

This is where I die... all because of fucking Elliott! Carmen cursed. Could she outrun them? Maybe she could throw the macaroni and cheese container, run to the Jeep, and hop in. Did she leave it unlocked? Where did she put the keys? *Shit! I don't remember.*

Momma bear inched closer, her nose mere inches from Carmen. Her ears flickered in surprise as she realized that there was a human in the hammock her cub was pawing. The shock turned to anger as she let out a loud growl and rose on her hind legs.

An answering roar from across the camp made Carmen jump and the bear hesitate. The momma bear swiveled on her hind legs toward the noise, a clumsy move that made her look nearly comical. She returned the roar, but her roar was weak in comparison. Whatever hovered in the bush was a much, much bigger predator. The cubs both ran to their mother, disappearing behind her.

The bushes parted and a creature stepped into the clearing. At first, she thought he was a tall, hairy man. He easily stood 7-feet-tall, with broad shoulders and thick, muscular legs. His body was covered entirely in curly, brown hair that thinned around his face to highlight a strong brow and small, expressive eyes. His large hands curled into fists at his side. His wide chest was covered in lighter, thinner hair that exposed the rippling muscle beneath.

He was naked and barefoot, with a significant male appendage between his legs. The creature let out another booming roar, his lips parting to show long protruding canines and sharp, carnivorous teeth.

She was going to die.

She scrambled out of the hammock, flipping it in the process. She landed on her ass, scraping her palms in her attempt to catch herself. She tried to push herself up and run, but where could she go? The bear cubs fled from behind their mother, disappearing into the opposite brush. The mama bear took one last look at the creature before she turned tail too, disappearing into the brush.

The creature watched them leave, his gaze unwavering until he was sure they were gone. He turned his eyes back to her. His expression was unreadable... but are people supposed to read an animal's facial expression? *Was this thing an animal?*He took a step toward her, pausing at the edge of her hammock. He knelt to pick something up from the ground under her hammock. He turned it over in his hands, examining it before brushing the dirt off it. He stepped over the hammock like it was a fallen log and crouched near her, holding the container of her macaroni and cheese toward her.

Her last thought before darkness overtook her was, *Is that Sasquatch?*

4

Carmen's eyelids flickered open, and she stared up into the face of the man.

Not a man, Sasquatch, her addled brain responded, trying to make sense of what she was seeing.

He knelt beside her, his thick brows furrowed as he stared down at her. She resisted the urge to run her fingers through the brown hair on his face, curious if it felt as soft as it looked. His eyes were a mahogany brown, almost black, and fixed on her with an expression that could only be described as concerned.

She jolted upward and skittered backward on her ass and palms, the dirt and rocks cut into her scraped palms. The man – beast, thing, whatever he was – didn't flinch. He just observed her with that same intent expression as she backed up against her Jeep and stood, her palms pressed against the car behind her. He rose, and she saw his full height. She'd been right earlier - easily seven feet. It wasn't that Carmen was short – she was a little over 5'6" – but he was impressively towering. Her eyes widened as he stood.

"Are you okay?" he asked.

He speaks! She could have fainted again in surprise. His gravelly voice was deep and scratchy, as if he were recovering from a terrible cold. He swiped his enormous hand over his face, and she noted the fur that covered his face and body extended onto the backs of his hands, stopping at his knuckles. His hands were human, which surprised her, although she didn't know why. What part of this made sense?

"Are you okay?" he repeated, his voice less scratchy this time. In his other hand, he awkwardly held her macaroni and cheese container.

"Uh... yeah," she said with a nod. She swallowed, her gaze darting around the campsite. *Where are my keys? Could I escape from him if I need to?*

He gave her cautious space, his movements slow. It didn't matter how slow and calm he was - he was built like a tree and *chased away a bear.* She glanced down at his naked lower half and cock. Her face reddened at her shamelessness. Her glance was quick but not too short to note that it was bigger than an ordinary man's. She hoped the moon wasn't bright enough for him to catch her looking.

If he noticed her glance, he said nothing. "You need

to keep food away. The bears will come." His cadence was different than anything she'd ever heard, his accent unplaceable. He emphasized the middle syllables of his words, tripping over the ends of them.

She knew she carelessly let herself fall asleep before securing the food. She knew better. She had a bear box, for fuck's sake! She just fell asleep. She hated the way men acted like she didn't know about hiking because she was a woman or that she wasn't as intelligent because of her skin color. The anger flared before she could tamp it down. Anger at Elliott, anger at being so stupid and breaking her own camping rules, anger at how this strange creature spoke to her.

"I know," she snapped. "I fell asleep; I know how to camp. I wouldn't have survived out here for the last few days if I didn't."

"Day," he corrected.

She blinked. "What?"

"Day, you've been here a day."

The memory of the flash of brown fur through the bushes came to her suddenly from that morning. "Are you *spying* on me?" she hissed. She almost took a step forward in confrontation, but her brain caught up with her anger and held fast.

Carmen was a bit of an exhibitionist. Her sexuality was one of Elliott's biggest complaints about her. She liked the thrill of maybe getting caught and the idea that at any moment, someone could walk in. Having sex in bathrooms at parties or cars before an event excited her, and she found the rush to be an immense turn-on. Elliott couldn't get over his ever-pressing fear of someone judging him to get into it.

They finally found something that worked for them both – role-playing. It wasn't any role-playing; it was a specific game. They'd meet at a bar or restaurant pretending to be strangers and order drinks for each other. It was a game of flirtation, a cat-and-mouse attraction to see who would cave first and demand they go home to have sex all night. Elliott liked the idea that he could pick up any girl in a bar and bring her to his bed; Carmen liked the idea of a brief encounter with a stranger. A perfect match, or so she thought.

No - being watched by a stranger while she masturbated didn't upset her. She was picking at things, trying to find a reason to be angry with the towering creature. She glanced down to his cock again, the bottom of her stomach churning in a familiar sensation of lust. It was a quick flash, pushed aside for some semblance of reason. Yes, this thing spoke like a man and looked like a man... but he was not human. This time he seemed to notice her looking; the edges of a smile twitched across his face.

"You're in my clearing," he simply said. He set the macaroni and cheese container on the ground near the rest of her stuff.

She raised her eyebrows. "Your clearing? I didn't

know you could own national parks." She crossed her arms over her chest.

He arched a furry brow. "National parks are made for me," he said, as though that made sense.

"What does that even mean?" she scoffed. She took a tentative step toward him, still keeping a safe distance if she needed to run.

"My people, we require peace. Privacy," he said the last word with a pointed look. "National Park promises this. Keeps us safe. This is my clearing."

"There's more of you?" she asked in a whisper.

He nodded and vaguely waved his hands. "Yes, many more, all over. This is my spot; it's... special."

The corners of his lips turned up faintly as he said the last word. She didn't understand what that meant, but she had the distinct impression he was talking about more than just a random spot near the river.

"Well, I'm sorry if I took your spot. I was given directions from a friend," she said.

His head tilted. "Who gave you?" he asked.

"My friend." She chewed her bottom lip, not wanting to give up Devan's identity. *Don't be ridiculous; it's not like he has a cell phone or computer in the bushes,* she chided herself. "I needed time to... clear my head."

"Does your friend have a name?" His face pulled into a full smile, the corners of his eyes crinkling.

"Devan."

"Yes, good, Devan."

"You know Devan?" Carmen asked.

"Very much," he said, his grin widening.

Between his legs his cock twitched. Her gaze darted to it, trying not to stare as it hardened.

How the hell did he know about Devan? Was he getting a boner talking about her?

Words rang in Carmen's memory: *The best way to get over someone is to get under someone else.*

Fuck! Isn't that what Devan told her with a wink while passing the instructions to the campsite? *Did Devan... did Devan have sex with this...sasquatch?*

The more she stared at him, the more she was reminded of her biology class in college, when they learned about the origin of man. He looked like... what was it? Gigantopithecus? A great, tall ape creature may have competed for resources with man. He wasn't as tall as them, maybe the product of their ancestors getting too friendly with Neanderthals? She didn't know; her mind spun, trying to make sense of what was before her. She wasn't a fucking expert in evolution.

He cleared his throat, turning his back to head toward the bushes.

"Wait," she said, suddenly not wanting him to go. She had so many questions, and not just about his heritage.

He paused at the edge of the clearing.

"Do you... do you want me to leave?" she asked hesitantly.

He blinked a few times and shook his head. "Stay, be careful." He glanced at the pile of her food sitting out in the moonlight.

"I... I will. Thanks, by the way. With the bears."

He lifted his shoulders in a shrug before disappearing into the night.

5

—————

Carmen wasn't sure if she should be frightened or comforted by his presence. Without knowing his name, she'd thought of him as Sasquatch, the mythical – or so she thought – creature that roamed the Rocky Mountain National Park. He more or less said he was part of a much bigger family with many others like him. That would explain the varied sighting of them over the years.

Sasquatch, Bigfoot - they were a local legend. She'd watched countless TV series and listened to podcasts over the years of so called hunters. The stores in Estes Park sold t-shirts with his likeness on it. He was a cryptid, a thing of mythology. She must have hit her head when she fell out of the hammock, there was no other reasonable explanation for his existence.

Carmen slept fitfully, her mind straying to the

darker and deeper implication of why she'd been given the directions to come here...

Devan. *Did Devan... did she fuck Sasquatch?* Did she tell Carmen about this place so Carmen might also sleep with Sasquatch? Sure - her friend sent her to a remote camping ground in a national park, the spot of choice for a mythical cryptid that saved her from being mauled by bears and then planned to fuck her brainless. She laughed to herself and tossed in her sleeping bag, shaking her head. Soon, her dreams turned to fantasies about the creature's gigantic hands on her breast.

SHE SEARCHED for him the next morning. It felt intrusive - she was in *his* clearing after all. Her gaze darted to the brush to look for his fur amongst the gaps. In the afternoon, she made lunch as she strained to listen for the sound of footsteps or the rustle of the bushes. She heard only by the sound of the wind in the trees and the birds chirping in the trees.

After a short hike to clear her head, she'd come to the conclusion she'd made it all up. Last night was clearly some sort of fever dream or the result of a concussion. Maybe she fell out of her hammock and hit her head while sleeping? She had bruises along her ass, her head hurt a bit, and gravel and dirt marked her palms. *Yes, this is only a weird hallucination dream thing.*

She hiked back to camp, stopping abruptly as she rounded the bend. *He* was in the tributary, his back to her. He dipped his hands into the stream, scooping water to splash over his head and body. The water made his fur cling to his skin, outlining his shapely ass. She still hadn't moved from her frozen position; her breath hitched in her throat as she gawked.

He turned, at last, not at all surprised to see her standing there. His gaze met hers across the clearing, burning with a ferocity he didn't have the night before.

She took a few tentative steps toward the camp, shedding her pack.

He watched her without a word, tracing her every move as she grabbed the hem of her shirt and peeled it off. It was the only time they broke eye contact, even as she unclasped the front of her sports bra and dropped it onto the ground. She moved toward the water, abandoning her shorts and panties. Last were her boots and socks, which she left on the edge of the tributary.

She barely felt the chill of the water as she continued toward him fully naked, doing nothing to hide herself. Her breath came in rapid gasps as she paused a few feet from him. She wasn't sure if it was the water's chillness or the sudden realization of what she was doing. Was she goading him, a potentially wild creature, with her nudity? Did she want something from him? It was the only way to appease her curiosity.

His gaze slowly raked up her body, starting at her exposed upper thigh just above the waterline, pausing around her pussy, then her breasts, and then her eyes again. He tilted his head ever so slightly as he assessed her.

She spoke first. "Devan gave me directions here because I'd just broken up with my boyfriend. Did she send me here because of you?"

He nodded, swallowing hard, his Adam's apple bobbing under his thick fur. He took a step toward her, testing her reaction. When she didn't back away, he took another step until he stood right in front of her. She tilted her head back to watch him, trying not to stare at his thick cock. It was primarily erect now and mere millimeters from pressing against her lower chest.

"I saw you," he said, tentatively reaching out to touch her hair.

Still, she didn't move, her eyelids fluttering at the touch.

His touch was soft and reverent as he ran his fingers through her curly strands. "I saw you in here. I saw..." His gaze glanced down her body, his tongue darting out to lick his lips.

So, he was watching me, she thought, surprised at

the sudden warmth that realization brought between her thighs.

His fingers were still in her hair, playing with its wisps while he regarded her with awe.

Elliott had never looked at her like this, she realized. Toward the end, he seemed annoyed, like anything she wanted to do was an inconvenience. He stopped wanting to play her games in bed; he stopped asking about her day. This strange beast of the woods made her heart lurch just by the look on his face.

"What's your name?" she asked.

His fingers stilled in her hair, and his gaze returned to her face. "You have a name for me," he said.

She shook her head. "What do you call yourself? What do your friends call you?"

He was quiet for a long moment, and she worried she'd upset him. He stiffened at her last question, his grip tightening on her hair. It only worked to speed up her already racing heart.

"Does no one..." she started, then stopped. "Well, does anyone..."

He took a step back, dropping her hair.

She reached out before he could get too far, her fingers closing on his wrist. "Wait, I just... I didn't mean to..." she lamely started. "I'm Carmen."

He stopped retreating, his eyes boring into her fingers on his wrist.

"Sam," he said, struggling over the word. "Some have called me... Sam."

Sam the Sasquatch. Carmen would have laughed if she weren't so worried he'd leave her alone with the growing ache between her legs.

"Okay, Sam," she said, her fingers still on his wrist. They were at an impasse; one had to do something, one would have to move, or this moment would pass.

Carmen acted first, her gaze dropping to his dick. It'd softened with whatever memory caused him to turn away from her. It looked very human, and it occurred to her that maybe he was human, maybe he just had a mutation. Hadn't she seen some documentary about how the werewolf kids in circuses had a genetic disorder that made them grow a bunch of hair? Another quick assessment shot down this theory; his body structure was too strange. He looked as if the strongman and the wolfwoman had made a kid.

He caught her looking at his cock, his lips twitching. She let go of his wrist and dropped to her knees. She knelt tenderly on the shore's sand, licking her lips as she observed his throbbing and growing cock. It was hardening again, extending to its impressive size. She moved forward to pass a tentative tongue along the tip, reveling how it jumped in excitement. She brought her hand to the base to wrap her fingers around it and brought her head forward, taking the full tip into her mouth. He groaned, or at least what she thought was a groan. It was guttural, more monster-like than human, and it shot a thrill through her.

His hands hesitantly went back to her hair, one twirling the curls between his fingers, the other resting on the top of her head to guide her pace. Before long, his cock was slick with her saliva and his pre-cum, her mouth moving quicker and steady with just the right amount of pressure as he guided her.

He was insistent but not aggressive, letting up when she backed off to take in air. She raked her teeth along the soft underside of his dick and his hand in her hair tighten just enough to send another jolt through her. His hand on her head moved to her jaw, a commanding move to pull her up to a standing position.

He stood over her with a carnal gaze as he looked down on her. Those blue-green eyes were alight with something monstrous, and she wondered what it would feel like to feel his beard against her thighs. She didn't need to wonder long. In one smooth motion, he'd picked her up and threw her over his shoulder. Carmen called out in surprise; she hadn't expected his movement. One hand rested at the junction of her ass and thigh, tightly gripping it. She bounced over his shoulder until he softly deposited her on the hood of her Jeep – just like in her fantasy.

He pushed her thighs apart as she rose onto her elbows to watch in fascination. He was bent before her, staring at her pussy like it was a prize. His hands roughly gripped her thighs, almost painfully tightening. He released one to trail it down the wetness of her pussy, prying her lips open to look deeper. His mouth was partially open, and she saw his large canines, his teeth that looked more suited for a carnivore than an omnivore like humans or apes. To her surprise, the thought thrilled her. *What would those teeth feel like biting into my flesh?*

Sam didn't hesitate; his mouth moved closer and closer to her wanting pussy. He started at the bottom near her ass, his tongue probing her open lips and bringing one into his mouth. He slowly sucked, pulling her open more. She groaned with need, longing for his tongue and mouth elsewhere. He was content to explore, though, letting go of her with a pop. Then it was the other side, his teeth gently exploring her tender flesh. She flinched, and he paused, looking up at her with worry. She nodded at him, her lip caught between her teeth.

He turned back to her, sliding his tongue into her waiting hole. Her head immediately fell back; what he did brought so much pleasure, but she craved something more. He was slow with his tongue, letting it lap at the juices flowing from her, then upward to her clit to circle and suck on it.

This was what she wanted. She bucked her hips at the sudden pressure and sensation, loudly groaning.

His hand slide up her thigh and insert one thick finger into her. It was the equivalent of two human fingers - thick, rough, hitting all the right spots as he advanced it in slow, languid movements. He alternated between sucking on her clit and licking it with the tip of his tongue.

The twin sensations of his mouth and tongue were nothing like she'd felt. Boyfriends in the past didn't understand the slow and steady building the way Sam did. Unrushed, he meticulously added a second finger, filling her with an almost painful fullness. Still, she egged him on, lewdly gyrating her hips against his hand.

She didn't care what she looked like, splayed over the hood of her Jeep open and exposed. All she cared about was the feeling of her orgasm building to a head quicker than she expected. He must have sensed that, felt the way she was pushing against him and urging him to move faster, to finger her harder. Sam complied and groaned that monster-like growl into her pussy. The vibrations traveled to her toes, pushing her orgasm to the forefront.

Sam didn't stop as she came, her head thrown back as she cried out. Her pussy clench over his fingers as he curled them inside her, her wetness running down his arm. His tongue didn't slow as he continued to flick and suck on her now overstimulated clit. Sam slowed as she came down, inching away from her clit as she shivered at any stimulation. He withdrew his fingers last.

Her eyes were closed, her head back against the hood of her Jeep. After a few deep breaths, she cracked them open and squinted into the sun to see him standing over her, watching, waiting, almost as if he was calculating his next move.

"Okay?" he asked. His already gravelly voice was deeper, thick with need. His eyes unabashedly roamed over her naked, splayed body.

"Very okay," she said with a laugh. Her eyes darted down to his cock. It hadn't shrunk while he was eating her out. It was even fuller, straining away from his body and toward her wet cunt. She sat up, reaching out to grab him.

He backed away, and she stopped, her gaze holding his.

"What?" she asked. "Do you not... want to?"

She wasn't sure what to ask about his hesitance. Was it some code he couldn't break? Part of his contract for living in the national park undisturbed? *Yeah, Sam, set up shop in the middle of nowhere but don't fuck the humans – strictly off limits.*

"Do you?" he asked, tilting his head left, then right.

She knew her question was silly. Of course, he wanted to fuck her. The way he still stared at her and his hands still roamed her body, tweaking a nipple between his fingers and reveling at her groans secured that he did. She could only nod her reply, loving the sensation of his rough, big fingers over her nipples. They'd always been so sensitive.

Sam didn't respond. Instead, he leaned forward to take a nipple in his mouth. At first, he sucked it like he did her clit; his tongue swirling over the tip with quick flicks. The flicks became more insistent before she felt his sharp teeth close gently over her nipple.

"Oh god, Sam," she groaned. Her hand landed on his neck, feeling the thick muscle under his hair. It was almost long enough to grab a handful in her fist. She dug her fingernails into his neck.

He moved to her other nipple and repeated his motions, drawing another strangled groan from her. She reached between them to grab his cock and lead it to her waiting pussy. He ran the length of it up and down her slit, covering it with the wetness and saliva from before.

Sam bit her nipple a little harder as he inserted the tip of his cock into her, stopping there. His fingers had prepared her for what was next as he slid into her bit by bit. He didn't stop licking and sucking and biting her nipples during this, and she did nothing to stop him, her fingernails digging harder and harder into his neck.

He eventually bottomed out in her, his balls bumping against her ass. He proceeded like that for a long moment before running his hand down to her stomach to press her flat on her back against the hood. His palm was splayed across her hips, digging into the soft flesh of her lower abdomen, holding her perfectly still while he slid in and out of her. His other hand grabbed her left ankle and brought it up to his shoulder, giving him deeper access to her.

Like everything else, he started slowly, bringing himself out nearly to the tip before pushing into her inch by inch. It was torturous, especially when he was entirely in her. She tried to ride back against him to speed him up, but his hand stayed put, forcing her still while he thrust in and out. His eyes were locked on her with that same feral expression, as though he were trying not to tear her into tiny pieces.

He could, she realized. Those small blunt horns on his forehead could easily knock her out. He was broad, and his muscles were visible beneath his body's fur. He could probably rip her arm off if he so wanted to. But instead of scaring her, this just thrilled her. The ultimate bad boy.

At long last, he sped up, his pace increasing exponentially with each thrust. His hand slid lower to finger her now recovered clit, his thumb moving over the hood, pressing on and circling it with each thrust. She felt the start of another orgasm building, this time faster, pressed on by the depth of his thrusts.

He adjusted her more, hauling her left leg higher up his chest. The sensation was overpowering this time. That was all it took for her to cum again. The tightness in her lower abdomen unfurled, and she came with a loud cry, arching her back off the hood.

Sam gave a few more thrusts before he buried himself all the way in her, making small, jerking thrusts as he came. He didn't let go of her leg until he finished, letting it drop back down to her side.

She panted as her heart raced, her body weak from cumming twice in such a short time. Had she ever orgasmed like that before? No, not with someone else, she realized. Sam slid from between her legs and she heard him disappear into the bushes a few minutes later, leaving her naked and spread on the hood of her Jeep, his cum pooling under her.

6

———

To her dismay, Carmen didn't see Sam for a few days. She worried she wouldn't see him again before leaving, which was only two short days away. It had been a week since she'd retreated to the woods; if she were gone longer, people would worry. As much as Carmen wanted to expand her trip and find him, she was resigned to the fact that he was probably done with her. He'd fucked her on her car's hood and immediately left. End of business transaction.

Even though she was sore for a full day afterward, she still longed for his touch again. The little bite marks on her breasts only reminded her of his tongue and mouth and sent chills down her spine. She considered trekking through the brush to find him but remembered the bears. Carmen was lucky enough for him to chase them away last time; she didn't think she'd get lucky again.

So, she spent the rest of her trip like she spent the first few days – swimming, sunning, and hiking. She curled into her hammock at night, read her steamy romance novel, and had to satisfy herself in between chapters. She was hornier than ever, masturbating two to three times a day. She did so out in the open, so he could see her if he was watching. She wanted him to swoop in and fuck her again, but the brush stayed silent.

THE NIGHT before she was set to leave, she saw him again. She was cooking up the last of her macaroni and cheese when she saw him watching her through the bushes. She jumped up in surprise, not expecting him to be standing there. He retreated into the brush before she could stop him.

"Wait, Sam!" she called. She threw her half-cooked meal into her bear box and took off after him through the bushes. At first, she lost him, but then some movement through the trees set her off at a jog deeper into the brush. She plowed through small bushes and trees, pushing their branches away from her. He was always just ahead of her, disappearing around the next bend.

She stumbled into a clearing and was shocked to see a cabin. It was made of logs and modest in size, but it was still a cabin in the middle of the woods. She hesitantly approached it, her fingers wrapping around the doorknob. She turned and pushed the door open, half expecting to see a group of park rangers sitting over their coffees. Instead, there was Sam. His enormous frame awkwardly stood in the middle of the room, his gaze trained on her as she stepped inside.

Across the space was a rudimentary kitchen with a bucket of water for a sink and some butane-style camping stove. Various pots, pans, and dishes were neatly stacked on wooden shelves on the wall. To the right of Sam, a cot made of blankets on the ground served as a makeshift bed. There were a few windows to give natural light and a fireplace against the far wall.

"You live here?" Carmen asked.

Sam gave one nod, then shrugged.

"Did you... build this?" she asked.

He gave another nod. "Some things I took," he said.

"Understandably." She assumed he was talking about the pots and pans and the bucket. She crossed the room to his bed and peered down at it.

"You sleep here?" she asked.

He nodded again, observing her.

"Is this where you've been hiding?" she asked.

He suddenly shook his head. "No hiding," he said. He wasn't a talented liar.

"Was I not good enough?" Carmen asked next, unable to keep the hurt from her voice.

He took a step toward her, his head shaking harder than before. "No, not very good. Very..." his eyes unabashedly raked her body. "Very good."

"Hmm," she said.

"Hmm?" he echoed. He moved toward her even as she retreated toward his bed.

She flopped down on it, surprised at how thick and soft it was. He gazed down at her, that same predatory look he had when he was deep in her on his face. She smiled wanly, leaning back on her elbows and spreading her knees. She was still fully clothed, but he looked at her like he did when she was nude and walking into that river after him.

"Then why have you been avoiding me?" she asked.

He sank to his knees in front of her, pushing her knees further apart to crawl between them. "Have not," he responded, fingers roaming up her thighs, cupping her through her shorts.

She groaned at the gesture, shaking her head. "Have too," she countered.

He didn't answer, just pushed her shorts and panties aside to slide a finger into her. She hissed out a breath. It wasn't out of pain; she was already wet. It was out of need.

"Hmm," he responded, slowly sliding his finger in and out of her. She chewed on her bottom lip, torn between calling him out on ghosting her and just enjoying the moment. She'd leave the next day. What was it she wanted? This was a fun fling, one getting more fun by the minute. Devan was right; the best way to get over someone was to get under someone else. She hadn't thought about Elliott in days!

Carmen reached for the bottom of her shirt, prying it off and throwing it onto the floor. Next, her fingers snagged the underside of her sports bra, peeling it off as quickly as possible. Sam watched her the whole time in silence, his fingers moving in that same slow motion. His thumb had moved up to her clit, gently pressuring it without actually moving. It was infuriating, just the ghost of his thumb against her hot skin.

His finger slid out of her, and he held it up between them, marveling at the wetness that stuck to it. He brought it to his mouth and sucked, groaning. Carmen took that moment to shimmy out of her shorts and panties, kicking them away with the same fervor as her top.

Sam pulled his wet fingers from his mouth and brought them down to her hips. He gripped them tightly, before flipping her over onto her hands and knees. His knee pressed into her inner thigh, spreading her wider. That finger slid back into her, pushing in and out with that frustratingly slow rhythm. She reached between her legs to rub her clit; if he wasn't going to, she might as well. She heard a noise that may have been a chuckle, but she wasn't sure.

He withdrew his wet finger and replaced it with the head of his cock. She sucked in a breath at the sensation, feeling it press hard against her opening. He continued to press, that same gentle pressure his fingers used, passing the thick head into her. The next few inches of his cock followed, stopping halfway in. He rocked it there, fucking her with slow, powerful strokes. He bent over to loop his hand around her, pressing his fingers against her clit. That was what she wanted! She let herself fall onto her elbows, ass up in the air as he pumped into her with small, slow strokes.

She always liked doggie style, especially with the wildly primal way he was fucking her. She came faster than she realized she could. The head of Sam's penis was hitting the perfect spot inside of her, sending bolts of electricity through her at every thrust. Coupled with his wet, thick fingers on her clit, she came undone, groaning into his mattress. He didn't stop fucking her, his strokes getting longer and faster.

She felt something wet trail across her ass cheek and rest between them, pooling at the hole there. Before she had time to work out what it was in her post-orgasm haze, she felt the strange pressure of Sam's wet finger probing her ass. At first, she started, unsure of what to do. She'd had nothing in there besides an occasional finger, and one of Sam's fingers was easily twice the thickness of a normal one. She didn't even remember if she liked it! Sam didn't stop despite her jerking, smearing the mix of her wetness and his pre-cum along that hole until it was just as wet as her pussy.

Sam slowed his strokes down just enough to focus on pressing that finger into her. At first, it was unforgiving; he pushed harder and harder into her unyielding hole. "Relax," he said. She tried to but couldn't shake the worry that he was going to put his dick in her ass. The thought of being filled like that was a confusing one, one she wasn't sure if she was into or not. There's no way she could take it... could she?

Still, he pressed, and her ass gave way to let him slide in his finger. He resumed his quicker pace, rocking into her pussy with his thick cock while his finger slid a few inches into her. He thrust it as a counter-movement; a cock in, finger out, cock out, finger in. It was a strange feeling that quickly gave way to pleasure. She felt full in a way she'd never been before, not painful or uncomfortable. Before long, she pushed back into him, his urgency increasing. He was close; she could tell by how his other hand gripped her hips and kneaded her ass cheek. Sam's fingers were strong and punishing, and she knew she'd have bruises, but she didn't care.

Carmen groaned as he came, feeling the weight of

his body as he leaned over her. He thrust a few more times before burying himself all the way in, his finger sliding to the inner-deepest part of her cavity. After a moment's rest, he pulled out of her, and she could feel the splash of his cum slide down her inner thigh. His finger retreated shortly afterward, and so did he. She heard him standing and walking away.

Anger coursed through her. *This again? Where would he even fucking go?* She was in his cabin!

When she noticed him rummaging through his things, she spun around, angry words on her tongue. She frowned, watching as he extracted something and made his way back to her. She watched his cock bounce between his legs, glistening with wetness, half erect. If he was upset that she was no longer on all fours, he said nothing, just resumed his spot between her legs. She caught sight of what was in his hands – a dildo.

"Where did you get that?" Carmen asked, fascinated.

He regarded the item, twirling it over in his hands. "Gift." He lowered the dildo to her pussy, sliding it along the cum that had collected along her thigh and what was slowly still sliding out of her. He was soaking the dildo in their wetness. It was slightly bigger than the average penis but still smaller than his own and was green.

To Carmen's surprise, he handed the soaked item

to her. Her fingers closed on the rubbery material, holding it out in front of her. What did he want her to do? Did he want to watch while she fucked herself with it? She didn't have time to ask; he was up again, looking around for another item.

Her surprise mounted when he returned with straps. At first, she didn't understand until she saw him unfurl them and then retrieved the dildo from her, placing it within the straps.

It's a strap on. She'd only seen them before in porn, a fact she was a little ashamed to admit. She had an old roommate in college who was really into watching porn. One weekend he went out of town, and curiosity got the better of her. She'd looked through his stash of videos on his hard drive, randomly picking a few and watching them. Some of them she hadn't liked; she could tell the women were faking it, and the positions and movements seemed unnatural and uncomfortable. Out of curiosity, she clicked on something she'd never heard before – pegging. The video opened to a woman with a strap on, fucking a guy with it as he was bent over the edge of the couch.

Sam handed her that exact item as though he were handing her a napkin or a fork. She warily held it in her hands, unsure what to do. "I haven't... I've never..." she started.

He nodded, though he didn't look the least bit upset or concerned.

She remembered the look on his face when he scared the bears away, and a shudder ran down her spine. If she said no, what would he do? She didn't think he would hurt her, but she wasn't sure what he was like when angry.

Instead, Sam helped Carmen to her feet, though he kneeled on the ground. He wrapped one strap between her legs and nestled it between her pussy's lips. Something made her gasp when he put a little pressure on her clit. He fed the strap between her ass cheeks, meeting the straps secured around her waist. After a few full tugs and pulls, it was on, and her green rubbery cock swung between her legs.

"There," Sam said as if that was the end of her concerns.

"You want me to..." She motioned to the rubber penis and then to him. He nodded, turning away from her to get on all fours just like she had done just a few minutes prior. She hesitated, moving forward to position the tip against his asshole. At first, Carmen was surprised at his similar anatomy, but then she chided herself. Why wouldn't he have all the same holes as a human man? He looked like one, kind of, well, mostly.

She swallowed and gently pressed the head of the dildo to his ass. She gripped the base of the dildo to give support, running the wet tip around in circles to lubricate it as he did for her. Satisfied, she mimicked the slow movements he'd used on her, she pushed the tip of the dildo into his ass with slow, constant pressure.

Sam groaned when the head popped through, the muscles along his back tensing. She stopped, worried she'd hurt him.

"Go," he said, his voice taking on that gravelly tone it did the last time they were together.

Lust, she realized. This is what he sounds like when he's horny out of his mind. The idea she did that to him pushed her on, feeding little bits of the rubbery cock at a time. Once she was halfway in, she withdrew, trying to imitate a thrust. It took a few tries to get the hang of it; it's not like she was the one usually thrusting.

Underneath her, Sam clutched the blankets that made up his bed. The back of his brown hands were thick with blue veins and tendons as he clamped down on the blankets. Carmen rocked faster, finding a rhythm with her thrusts. She found with obvious pleasure that the flat base of the dildo would press against her clit, and the tug and pull of the straps caused enjoyable friction along her pussy and ass. It wasn't enough to make her cum, but it was enough to start the low hum of pleasure in her abdomen.

Carmen thought about reaching around to grab Sam's cock and jerk him off simultaneously, but he was too large for that. There's no way she could reach and thrust. As if reading her mind, Sam unfurled one of his hands and grabbed his dick, stroking it in time with her thrusts. She was all the way in now, burying her rubbery cock to the base with each thrust, bringing it almost to the tip before diving in again. She'd pause at the end, pushing against the flat base and enjoying the sensation of it over her clit.

Below her, Sam's hand moved faster and faster on his cock. She sped up to match, no longer going for the long, deep strokes. She found her new rhythm with fast, shallow ones, building up to a frenzy. She felt him tense before he let out a loud moan, his body shuddering with the force of his orgasm. He pumped his cock a few more times, his back rising and falling with his labored breathing.

Carmen slid the dildo out of his ass, detaching the straps, and discarded it next to the bed. She crawled into the bed next to Sam, carefully avoiding the pile of cum he'd left under him. Sam grabbed the top blanket with the cum and balled it up, tossing it off the bed. He reached out to grab Carmen by the waist, pulling her down beside him in bed.

Sam positioned himself behind her in a sort of spoon-like position, which was strange given their height difference. He pulled her close, nestling his softening dick against the crack of her ass. She realized then how exhausted she was and let her eyes flutter closed, falling asleep.

7

———

Carmen awoke to the feel of a large, warm hand on her hip and something equally warm and firm between her legs. Was she seriously a little spoon to Sasquatch? She blinked awake, stretching and reveling in the feel of her back popping. She was delightfully sore from both hiking and sex. The hand on her hip tightened as she stretched and unintentionally rubbed against the firm cock nestled against her ass.

The hand on her hip released its grip, traveling up her side and finally resting on her breast. Sam's fingers closed on her nipple, pulling and kneading until they were peaked, and her breathing picked up. She felt his cock twitch against her ass as he rocked, sliding it between her thighs. She was still wet from earlier, and it was coating his dick, mixing with the new wave of arousal she was feeling at his ministrations.

She felt his face press into the crook of her neck, his warm breath exhaling in rhythm with his slow thrusts. She lifted her hand to reach around his neck, pressing his face harder into her. She felt his sharp teeth prick the edges of her skin, sending a shiver down her spine. *What would it be like if he bit me?* He groaned into her neck, lifting his head slightly to catch her earlobe in his mouth and bite down. It was a sharp, painful sensation that he followed with gentle sucking as if kissing it to make it feel better.

His hand left her breast, traveling back down her side to her leg. He wrapped his arm under it, lifting her leg to pull her legs apart. With some maneuvering of his hips, he slid his stiff cock into her wanting, wet pussy. They groaned as he continued to drive his hips forward, stopping only when he was all the way in and paused. His chest rapidly rose and fell against her back. She was panting herself; she'd never been so quickly turned on.

His hand stayed hitched under her leg as he thrust. He didn't go as slow as he did before; he picked up speed. She pushed back against him, loving the feel and depth with her leg up like that. It gave her access to play with her clit, rubbing it slowly with her left hand as he continued to fuck her from behind.

Carmen felt his lips against her shoulder; she felt

the prick of his sharp teeth against her skin, a welcome surprise. His lips part against her shoulder and his teeth sink into her skin as he bit her, groaning loudly at this.

"Holy fuck," she hissed between her teeth, rolling her head back.

She was so close to cumming when he abruptly stopped. The hand on her leg tightened, his grip relentless as he threw her onto her back under him. Sam grabbed one blanket from the bed and rolled it up, shoving it under her hips to elevate her ass off the bed. He grabbed his cock to line it up with her and thrust in quickly, again abandoning his historically slow starting pace. He grabbed her left ankle and pulled it up against his chest, giving even more access to her, driving himself deeper as he thrust.

Sam's eyes fixated on her breasts as they bounced with every thrust, his hand tight on her ankle where it fell against his chest. Carmen returned to playing with her clit, this time with more insistence, as she chased that sensation of her orgasm again. She was so close before she huffed with anger at having to start again. His gaze lowered to watch her circle and strum her clit, his eyes glazed over in lust watching her.

It wasn't long until Carmen felt her orgasm curl in her stomach, her open mouth panting, turning into little moans every time he thrust into her. Her fingers moved quicker across her clit with more purpose, her hips jerking up to meet him as her orgasm took over. She closed her eyes, her fingers slowing as the sensations rolled through her. Her muscles tightened over his cock, gripping him as she came in waves. His fingers dug into her ankle, his moan drowning her out.

He didn't slow his thrusts as she came on his dick. Instead, he sped up, his other hand gripping her hip to help fuck her harder. He wasn't far behind her; after a few quick strokes, he buried himself thoroughly, his head tilted back as he came. His eyes closed, and his hips stuttered as he gave a few more small thrusts.

Carmen was panting, her eyelid heavy as she watched him sink back on his haunches, his half-erect cock slipping from her with an obscene squelch. He looked down at her, his mouth partially open as he panted.

Well... maybe Carmen could stay one more night.

LEAVING the campsite was like leaving a piece of herself behind. Carmen packed the last of her things, adjusting them in the back of her Jeep. She'd left Sam in the cabin after an awkward goodbye. He didn't seem upset to see her go; she'd gleaned from her visit that she was neither the first nor the last person to get the directions to Sam's campsite.

She knew this was a weekend fling, the type you read about in saucy novels by the beach. That didn't mean it didn't affect her or that she didn't come away with a new appreciation for what sex could be and feel like. If a creature she previously thought was a myth could bring her to orgasm quicker than she could herself, well... there was a fully human man out there somewhere who could fit that criterion.

Carmen closed the trunk door to her Jeep and cast one last glance toward the brush. She wasn't surprised to see Sam standing there, watching her go with an impassive look on his face. She raised her hand to wave goodbye. He returned the gesture with a small, gentle smile.

All she could think as she steered her Jeep down the bumpy road was, *Did I peg Sasquatch?*

THANK you for reading the first installment in *The Cryptids of America*, a series of novellas and short stories about the strange beasts that exist in America! Sam is the first of many monsters, creatures, and myths we'll meet over the series. Each story features a different main character from various backgrounds, with multiple interests and sexual encounters. You may want to stick around if Carmen and Sam aren't your speed. How about sapphic mermaids, a tentacled woman or a nonbinary forest god?

If you want additional chapters or to be informed of future releases, check out my website and subscribe to my newsletter. This gets you access to all sorts of goodies, like a chapter from Sam's POV! The website can be found at cm-deer.com/kll.

Be sure to follow me on Instagram and TikTok for teasers and more! My username is the same on both, katrynalalock.

ABOUT THE AUTHOR

I often get asked, "Katryna, how did you come up with the idea for the Cryptids of America series?" The answer is simple; I was window shopping in Estes Park when I saw the plethora of Sasquatch merchandise, and I wondered would he would be DTF?

That's how I come up with all my ideas; I see something and think, "Man, what a wild story THAT would be." Then I look it up and see there isn't a story like that, get bummed... then fire up the old Mac and get to typing.

The Cryptids of America is written as a series of shorts that can be read in any order, the only purpose is to make your toes curl and your mother blush. I exclusively write stories with action in them; no fade to black here, but the focus of the stories varies. Other stories I write aren't the same - some are longer forms where the smut is just an added bonus.

To keep up with the latest releases, special editions, and bonus chapters, my website and newsletter are fantastic resources at cm-deer.com/kll.

Mitch and Tatiana's love was all dried up.

They moved to the Pine Barrens with one goal: capture evidence of the Jersey Devil. The evidence they received from an anonymous listener of their podcast - CryptidCore99 - was all they had to go on when they packed up their life and moved to the woods. A year later they had nothing to show for it except a crumbling relationship. With just a week left before their lease is up and they part ways, things are looking dire.

At least, until Tatiana runs into the Jersey Devil on a run.

Sexual tension runs high when The Jersey Devil finds

sketches of himself in interesting positions with humans in Mitch's backpack. Is this encounter exactly what this couple needed to reignite their spark? Or is this the final straw that breaks them apart?

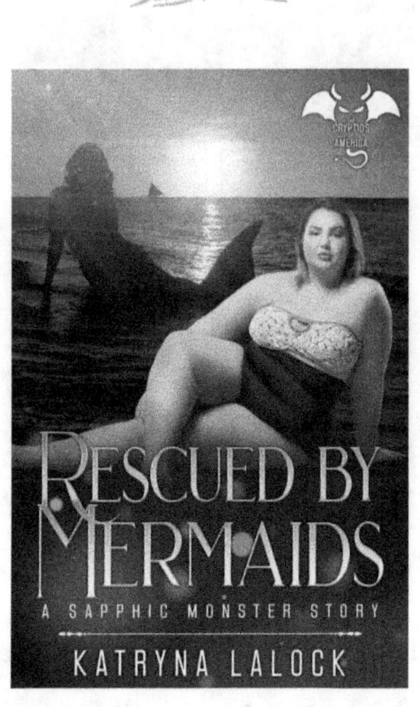

Hannah is lost on the ocean all because of a stupid work bet. If she hadn't let her stupid male coworkers upset her so much she wouldn't be in this position. It's day two lost off the shores of Florida and it looks like she's not going to survive this. She sings to pass the time, drawing the attention of a beautiful mermaid who rescues her and nurses her to health. Gabriella is beautiful and genuinely cares for Hannah. It doesn't take long for Hannah to fall in love with the dark haired beauty and her talented tongue.

Does Hannah even want to go back to the shore?

There were two creatures in this forest - one a god, one a monster. I was hunting the monster.

The forest god we worshiped for years may have given up on us, but I have not. After Greta was killed I vowed to stop the beast myself. I wasn't alone in the forest that night - our forest god watched. And once the beast was gone, I was the only creature they wanted.

When Melody's determination to explore the human world found her wandering the boardwalk against her ancestors' warnings, she wasn't looking for trouble – it just found her. Now, she's stuck in human form, searching for her seal skin and reluctantly accepting that her elders' fears may not have been so silly after all.

Life hasn't exactly panned out the way Addison had in mind. Job-hopping, living with roommates, and being stuck with a raggedy car that barely gets her anywhere wasn't precisely her idea of 'terrific thirties.' But going with the flow is all Addison knows, and a fateful night under the pier is all it takes for two unsuspecting souls to intertwine.

What should have been a simple search mission transforms into a not-so-simple entanglement neither Addison nor

Melody saw coming. And by the time Addison makes sense of her true feelings, she does the unthinkable – a decision that could cost her more than she imagined.

RESCUED BY MERMAIDS

A FF MONSTERFUCKER EROTICA

"**ARE YOU FUCKING KIDDING ME?!**" I screamed into the empty air. It was all open space, just water, no land or boats in sight.

As much as I would like to blame the guys at work, this was all my fault. I let their taunting get to my head and my Too Much gene kicked in. It started innocently enough, as most shitty work interactions do. We were headed for a conference in some part of Florida (I had no idea where; Florida was a wasteland as far as I knew.). We were a group of heads of departments as well as a few underlings. Honestly, it was just an excuse for most of them to get away from their kids and cheat on their wives. I'd heard these conferences were more like parties than actual places to learn.

I went because I was new to the company and I actually *did* want to learn a little bit and network. The company I'd joined wasn't what I wanted out of life; it was more of a stepping stone. I was hoping that this networking event would give me the means to go literally anywhere else. I hated the frat bro culture most of all. It was a man's world and I had the distinct impression that I was hired to fit some diversity requirement. Diversity to them being a white woman.

So, I went to this conference in tropical ass, humid as hell Florida. I went to the meetings and met people and networked and generally avoided my crew. I lasted a whole two days before the guys at work started in on The Race.

Apparently, at the end of the conference, there was a race. It was unsanctioned and involved a ton of alcohol. Each company put together a relay team of four rowers that would row around some inlet off the beaten path. It was a private beach owned by some mega-millionaire in the area, someplace everyone could get absolutely shit-faced and navigate boats with no risks of being caught or arrested for a DUI.

I found out about it tangentially, while they were talking about it at breakfast on the second to last morning. They were all obviously hung over, wearing thick sunglasses and struggling to keep down their waters. I was sitting at our table enjoying my own breakfast while reading a book when they plopped down around me one at a time, staring bleakly at the burnt toast on their plate. They immediately started to talk about the race and who they'd recruit this year.

"Hannah," said Ted, one of the HR reps. I tried to pretend like I hadn't been eavesdropping. This was the first I'd heard of any sort of race and my interest was piqued.

I didn't see it on the agenda. It must have been invite-only, I reasoned. "Hmm?" I asked, swallowing the last piece of my bacon.

"Nah," said Mike from accounting. "I don't think she'd be interested." He said it with a cursory look up and down my body. Ah, the age-old 'fat girl can't do sports.' I picked up another piece of bacon despite not actually being hungry anymore. It was a matter of principle at this point.

"Interested in what?" I asked with the same air of indifference. The guys exchanged glances, one of them openly glaring at Ted.

"It's a boat race," said Ted. "A rowing competition, actually. It's between all the companies, very competitive." The others around the table murmured their agreement.

"Nothing you'd be interested in," said another. He was one of the faceless guys from...sales? I didn't remember, they all kinda looked the same.

"Why wouldn't I be interested?" I asked innocently. I wanted to see if any of them had the balls to say what they were really thinking. It was no surprise to me when they exchanged glances again.

"It's just..." sales boy continued, steepling his fingers. "It's very...strenuous. It involves a lot of skill, too. I just don't see you being particularly interested. It's why we never mentioned it before today."

The truth is I *was* interested. I'd never rowed a day in my life, I wasn't a particularly strong swimmer, and the idea of competing alongside any of these chuckle-fucks made me want to throw myself off a cliff. Despite this, I could feel my common sense slipping away. The need to prove myself as a worthy member of their group was burning me up inside. Before I could stop them, the words poured out of my mouth; "I was captain of my undergrad crew team," I lied. I have no idea why I said it. It was an outright lie. It's not like I wasn't an athlete, I was just more of a runner to be honest. I'd done my share of 5k races and half marathons. Nothing about the open water appealed to me.

"You're kidding," said Mike. His tone implied that he truly didn't believe me. "Didn't you go to Arizona State University?" asked the sales fucker.

"There's a big canal system," I said. There was, but they weren't the type you'd row down. "And Tempe Town Lake," I added. "Very popular place for rowing. We also had the Salt River. Honestly, it's like you guys don't know anything about competitive crew." I popped another piece of bacon in my mouth and turned back to my book.

I watched them from the corner of my eye as they chatted under their breath. I caught bits and pieces here and there— "We can't let MegaCorp beat us again," and "Every year they taunt us relentlessly…"

At last, they made a decision and elected Mike to deliver it. "We'll have a little test run tomorrow morning. You know, to make sure you're up to snuff."

Like the dumbass I was, I was elated. I skipped the afternoon meetings to head a few miles down the shoreline to a kayak rental place. It was harder than I realized, and YouTube was only so useful. I rowed and rowed and…I must have hit a riptide or current or something like that because all of a sudden, I couldn't control my kayak. It was too strong and my sad little kayak was floating further and further away from the shoreline. I watched it disappear and, no matter how hard I rowed, I couldn't make up the distance.

So I tried to row a different way, seeing if I could get myself out of the current before turning to head back to shore. I turned and fought and eventually was free of it. I sighed in relief, sweating like a fucking pig in the process. The humidity was bad enough without the exertion of rowing. I may have run my share of races but those didn't really require upper body strength. I was exhausted and could only tread water for a while before I realized I was absolutely lost with no idea of where the shore was.

The panic at that realization was instant. I felt the tell-tale signs of an anxiety attack starting at my toes, tingling its way along my arms. My chest was heavy, I was short of breath and I was convinced that, if I didn't tell myself to breathe, I would stop and drop dead there. All the tactics my therapist gave me to work through these attacks flew out of my mind. It was replaced by the headline, 'Tourist Lost at Sea Trying to Prove Herself Like an Idiot to her Coworkers.'

It felt like hours before I finally calmed down enough to try to devise a plan. That was my strength, wasn't it? I was a problem solver, that's why I'd been hired by the company. I fixed things. I could fix this. The sun rises in the east and sets in the west... Where was the sun now?

Directly overhead. Shit.

Okay, so I could just wait a little bit for the sun to start to set then I could follow its trajectory. I was pretty sure I was on the east side of Florida, so I just needed to head west. It occurred to me then that the sun didn't set *exactly* west, it depended on the time of the year. That's why at Cichchen-Itza the sun only made that cool snake shadow twice a year on the solstices. Would it be setting west enough for me to find my way back to shore?

Shit, shit, shit.

This was my fault. If I didn't lie, if I didn't want so deeply to be liked by coworkers I didn't even care about, I would be at the conference sitting cozy, networking with a company that might actually take me seriously. I could blame the guys for treating me like shit and making me go to extremes to fit in, but at the end of the day, the only person I had to blame was myself.

So I stood up in the swaying kayak and screamed into the void, "ARE YOU FUCKING KIDDING ME?"

The ocean didn't respond.

The sun started to set and I followed the path.

What else could I do? I took a deep breath and put the rowers into the water, aware of how much heavier they felt than they did just a few hours ago. I gave a few quick strokes before I had to slow my pace. Follow the sun, follow the sun, follow the sun...

The sun set and I still didn't see shore. There was no way I was that far away. The rip tide couldn't have carried me so far away that I couldn't make it back within thirty, forty minutes tops. Plus...I didn't even *see* the shore. It wasn't like it was getting farther and farther away, it's that it just wasn't there. Night settled and the full moon shone over the waters, making the stars reflect along the surface. It was beautiful but I didn't give two shits. The rising panic I'd felt all day was at an ultimate head right now. I felt strung out, frayed at the edges, like pieces of me had been chipped off all day. My skin was sunburnt, my lips were chapped and I knew if I didn't get water soon, I'd die.

At least the moon brought some reprieve from the heat. The waters were almost chilly and I curled my arms around myself, sinking into the bottom of the kayak. *What do I do now?* I thought. I had no anchor, so my kayak was likely to float in whatever direction the waves drove it. Did I want that? Would it push me closer to land? I tried to think of that as a happy thought. Maybe I'd wake up and the shore would be just there on the edge of the waters. I'd be close enough for cell phone signal at least! *Yeah,* I told myself, *I'll wake up and the shore will be there.* Isn't that how waves work?

But it wasn't.

And by the time the sun was right above me again with no shore in sight, I knew I was going to die.

With acceptance came a sort of hysterical calm. Who cared if the kayak was floating? I was going to die anyway. Who cared that I hadn't seen a single helicopter or boat trying to find me? I was going to die anyway. It was a constant string of unintelligible thoughts, *Who cares anyway? I'm a dead woman floating.*

I'd removed my shirt and put it over my head for some semblance of protection. Occasionally, I'd dip it into the water to cool it off, keeping a steady stream on my body. I felt the salt dry on my skin and I realized in horror that I was no longer sweating. This was it. This was the end.

So I sang.

It may seem silly, but singing was a hobby of mine. I was always in choir and sang in church until I stopped being interested in religion. In undergrad, I sang in a few theatre shows and even minored in music. It was the type of hobby that was so precious you didn't want to monetize, didn't want to ruin it by trying to make it into a career, or use it to show off. I sang for myself and myself alone.

I hung over the edge of the kayak, my fingers trailing in the water, the sun beating down on my now exposed back, and I sang. I sang a full catalog of shit, too, popular tracks, opera, even church hymns. I considered it my finale, the encore really. No one would ever hear me sing again.

Well, except whatever it was that was moving under the water.

At first, I thought it was a figment of my addled brain. It was the size of a dolphin and swam in a similar way, its fin kicking below the surface. It was blurry and dark under the water, a form that was moving back and forth too consistently to be fake. I wondered vaguely if I could kill it and eat it, but then how would I cook it? Would eating some raw fish really save my life? Doubtful, it would just prolong the inevitable.

My throat felt dry and scratchy, my voice was faltering. I tried to think what I could sing that would be the perfect finale, the best song to play at my funeral. Funny enough, the only song I could think of was *Pursuit of Happiness* by Kid Kudi. So I sang that until my voice officially gave out, until the sun set and the moon was overhead again.

I felt the last bit of energy leave my body and I thought, *Thank god, I won't be awake for the end.* I could just slip into beautiful unconsciousness and not be aware of any of it. Below me, the large dolphin fish continued to swim back and forth, quicker now, irritable. It was getting closer to the surface, stroke by stroke.

Have you ever read Into the Wild? It's about a kid who decides to travel the US with nothing. It's something they made us read in high school. I'm not sure why, it was a complete counter to what they were pushing back then. This kid gave up everything and just lived life, abandoning college and responsibility to be free. Well...until he died in a bus alone in the Alaskan wilderness.

Some theories say he ate some potato seed and died. Others talked about hallucinations, about how he may have imagined and seen things that weren't really there in the end.

Surely—surely—this was what was happening to me now.

Because the last thing I saw before my body gave up and my eyes closed was a human face looking up at me from beneath the water.